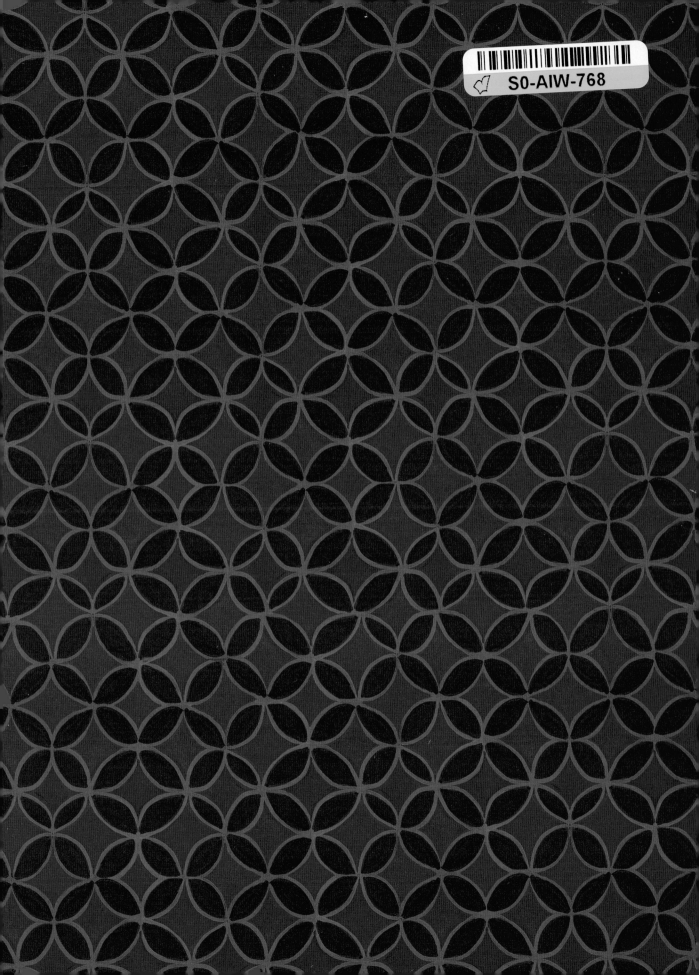

The Jade Necklace

For Jasmine Wong Denike — P.Y.
To Robert, who loves Canada — G.L.

Special thanks to the Vancouver Museum and its curator for exhibitions, Joan Seidl,
and Aniko Kis for archival photographic assistance.
Thanks also to Jane Li of St. George's School, Marie Leaf, Evan Lin, Everett Lin and Jay Wang
for editorial assistance with the Chinese characters.

First American edition published in 2002 by
CROCODILE BOOKS
An imprint of Interlink Publishing Group, Inc.
99 Seventh Avenue, Brooklyn, New York 11215 and
46 Crosby Street, Northampton, Massachusetts 01060
www.interlinkbooks.com

Published simultaneously in 2002 in Great Britain and Canada by Tradewind Books

Text copyright © Paul Yee 2002
Illustrations copyright © Grace Lin 2002

Book design, hand-lettering, and seals by Elisa Gutiérrez

Library of Congress Cataloging-in-Publication Data
Yee, Paul.
    The jade necklace / by Paul Yee ; illustrator, Grace Lin.-- 1st
American ed.
    p. cm.
    Summary: When her father is lost at sea during a typhoon and her
family no longer has enough to eat, Yenyee travels to Vancouver as a
servant, across the ocean which she feels betrayed her.
    ISBN 1-56656-455-7
    [1. Family life--China--Fiction. 2. Ocean--Fiction. 3.
Immigrants--Canada--Fiction. 4. Chinese--Canada--Fiction. 5. Vancouver
(B.C.)--Fiction. 6. China--History--19th century--Fiction.] I. Lin,
Grace, ill. II. Title.
    PZ7.Y365 Jad 2001
    [Fic]--dc21
                                    2001006496

Printed in Hong Kong

To request our complete 48-page full-color catalog,
please call us toll free at 1-800-238-LINK, visit our
website at www.interlinkbooks.com, or write to
Interlink Publishing
46 Crosby Street, Northampton, MA 01060-1804
E-mail: info@interlinkbooks.com

THE JADE NECKLACE

BY
PAUL
YEE

ILLUSTRATED BY
GRACE
LIN

Crocodile Books, USA

An imprint of Interlink Publishing Group, Inc.

New York • Northampton

When Yenyee was young, her fisherman father gave her a jade pendant that was carved like a fish with wavy scales, thin fins, and wide eyes. "This small gift comes from me and your friend, the sea," announced Ba.

Yenyee's face lit up like a candle. She fastened the necklace around her neck and vowed to never take it off. Toying with it, she mused, "The stone is land, and the fish is sea. What about the sky rolling over me?"

Her mother heard and said, "Well, sunshine bakes the jade, winds cool it, and moonlight gives it a silvery glow."

One day a typhoon hurled winds and rains at the coast. Dark clouds battled high above, while waves pummeled the docks and fishnets on the beach. Alone, Yenyee waited and wept in the rain. Her father's boat was nowhere to be seen.

She yanked the jade fish from her neck and shouted at the sky, "Oh Heaven, if I give you my most precious possession, please will you give me back my father?" And she flung the jade necklace into the swirling depths of the sea.

But Ba's boat did not return.

She turned her back on the ocean and vowed angrily, "Never again will you steal a loved one from me!"

寙
貧

Without Ba, without a boat, without fish to sell, Yenyee and her little brother went hungry. To raise some money, Ma sold the nets and sails, and even traded away her iron cooking pots. But soon the family was hungry again. Ma went behind the house, where Yenyee sat huddled into herself.

Ma placed her gold earrings in Yenyee's cold hands and said, "Daughter, go to Chen Ming and trade these for rice and fish."

Yenyee nodded, then walked to the market without once looking at the ocean.

Chen Ming, the merchant, greeted her warmly. "Yenyee, tell your mother I grieve for your loss. Your father was a fine man."

The girl pushed the gold earrings forward. "Ma says we need fish and rice."

"Yenyee," the merchant added, "I am moving my family to the New World. My daughter May-jen needs someone to care for her. Would you work for us?"

She replied, "I'll ask my mother."

Chen Ming pushed the earrings back to her and handed over rice, vegetables, and fish. "We leave next week," he said.

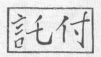

Reluctantly, Ma agreed to let Yenyee go. She tied extra clothing into a carrying cloth and said, "Daughter, Chen Ming has treated us kindly, so you must take good care of May-jen, even learn to love her. Do your job well, and then perhaps our family will reunite one day. Now promise me that you will not be afraid of anything."

Yenyee nodded and turned away so Ma wouldn't see her tears.

After several days at sea, a great storm arose. The ship tossed and rolled, the floor tilted from one side to the other, and the baggage slid back and forth. This terrified little May-jen. "The ship is sinking and we'll all drown tonight!" she screamed.

Yenyee remembered her words to Ma and to the ocean, but all she could do was pull May-jen close and murmur, "Don't worry about the sea. You're safe on this ship."

Gently she hummed fishing songs that her father used to sing, and May-jen fell asleep while high waves flattened.

In the New World, May-jen fell silent, afraid to make mistakes in English. Learning a new language, she struggled with her homework and felt the teacher was always frowning at her. When schoolmates approached her, she backed away fearfully. She dreaded going to school and ran home alone every day with her books.

In the mornings, when Yenyee braided May-jen's hair and tied it firmly with bright red string, she noticed sad eyes and trembling lips. She put an arm around the little girl and said gently, "Don't worry, the hurt will disappear. Soon we'll both feel better."

In fact, both girls craved things beyond their reach. They wanted to hear the hearty shouts of peddlers in the market, smell salty treats being fried in the open air, and taste banana candies that were harder than rock. May-jen wanted to play with her former friends, and Yenyee wanted to see the glowing faces of her mother and brother. But all she could do was pray for their well-being.

且力友

One weekend, two girls visited Chen Ming's store and asked if May-jen would join in a game of jump rope. Chen Ming called for May-jen, but she refused to come. After the disappointed playmates left, the merchant turned to Yenyee, "What can be done to cheer up my little girl?"

She thought for a moment. "What if I take her to the park? I've heard there's lots to see."

The two girls took the tram to Stanley Park and strolled along the seawall. Yenyee would have avoided the ocean altogether, but May-jen wanted to smell the salty air up close. The faraway horizon and ships seemed close enough to touch. Ocean winds blew fresh and strong, and above them seagulls soared. Yenyee's thoughts flew among them to a faraway yet familiar beach where her mother and brother called to her over the waves.

Suddenly a bicycle sped by. When May-jen jumped aside, her hat flew off. Reaching for it, she lost her balance and fell into the water! It happened so fast that Yenyee thought she was dreaming. "May-jen!" she shouted. "Where are you?"

Although the water swirled like murky ink, Yenyee jumped straight in. The cold jolted her. She tasted salt water and felt the current pulling, but her arms and legs moved on their own. She peered into the gloomy water, but saw nothing. Then a glimmer of red flashed. It was fine string coiled around a braid.

Yenyee grabbed the braid with one hand and kicked upward. She finally broke the surface, and the two girls gasped for air. Helpful hands were there reaching for them.

Back on the seawall, May-jen coughed and coughed. Then she burst into tears, "You saved my life!"

Yenyee hugged her tightly. Strands of milky-green seaweed clung to the arms and legs of the two girls. They tore them off, laughing and crying at the same time. Then May-jen's fingers caught something tangled in Yenyee's hair. She pulled, and out came the jade fish, the pendant from her Ba, hanging on the cord that once looped around her neck. Yenyee stared at the jade necklace, then at the churning waters below. She looked toward the horizon. On the other side of the ocean lay all her memories. The waves foamed, and the glistening surface seemed solid enough to walk on.

"Thank you, Mighty Ocean," she whispered. "I won't be angry at you anymore."

When the two girls arrived home, May-jen ran ahead to tell her father what had happened. A warming fire was lit as Chen Ming hugged both girls.

"How can I ever thank you?" he asked Yenyee.

She hesitated for a moment and glanced at May-jen, happily wrapped in her father's arms. Then Yenyee declared, "By bringing my mother and brother here to live with me!"

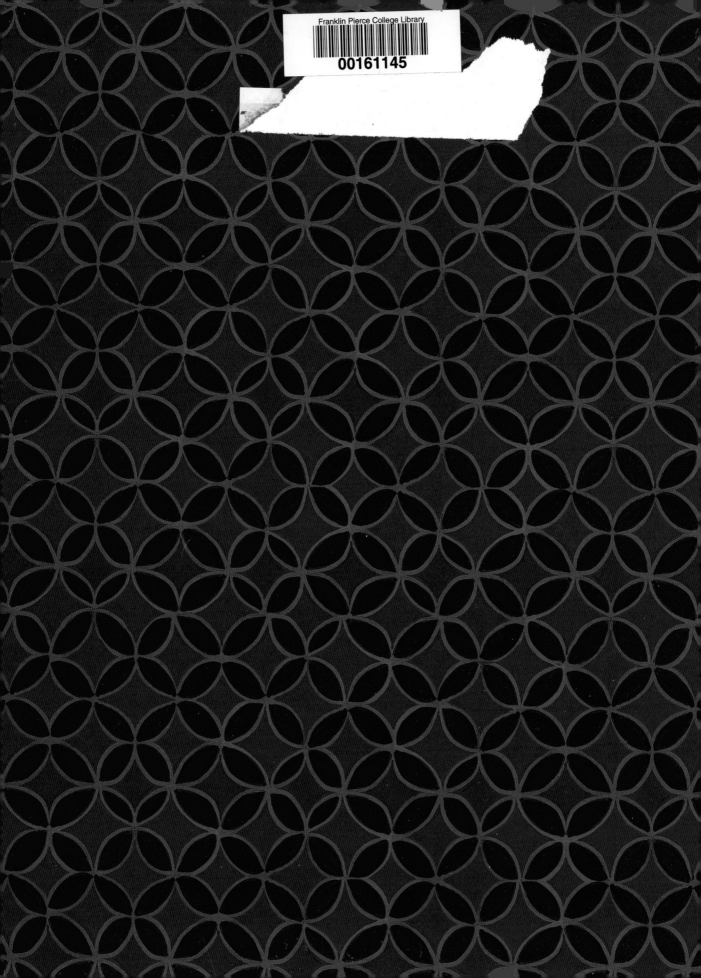